S0-DTD-389

The Black Kitten

by
W.G. Van de Hulst

illustrated by
Willem G. Van de Hulst, Jr.

INHERITANCE PUBLICATIONS
NEERLANDIA, ALBERTA, CANADA
PELLA, IOWA, U.S.A.

Library and Archives Canada Cataloguing in Publication
Hulst, W. G. van de (Willem Gerrit), 1879-1963
[Zwarte poesje. English]
The black kitten / by W.G. Van de Hulst ; illustrated by
Willem G. Van de Hulst, Jr. ; [translated by Harry der Nederlanden].
(Stories children love ; 7)
Translation of: Het zwarte poesje.
Originally published: St. Catharines, Ontario : Paideia Press, 1979.
ISBN 978-1-928136-07-1 (pbk.)
    I. Hulst, Willem G. van de (Willem Gerrit), 1917-, illustrator
II. Nederlanden, Harry der, translator III. Title. IV. Title: Zwarte
poesje. English V. Series: Hulst, W. G. van de (Willem Gerrit), 1879-1963
Stories children love ; 7
PZ7.H873985Bla 2014   j839.313'62   C2014-903600-0

Library of Congress Cataloging-in-Publication Data
Hulst, W. G. van de (Willem Gerrit), 1879-1963.
[Zwarte poesje. English.]
The black kitten / by W.G. Van de Hulst ; illustrated by Willem G. Van de Hulst, Jr. ; edited
by Paulina Janssen.
pages cm. — (Stories children love ; #7)
"Originally published in Dutch as Het Zwarte Poesje. Original translation done by Harry
der Nederlanden for Paideia Press, St. Catharines-Ontario-Canada."
Summary: Sandy rescues a kitten from falling into freezing water but a passerby thinks
she is trying to drown the kitten instead, and to make things worse, getting wet causes
Sandy to become very sick.
ISBN 978-1-928136-07-1
  [1. Animal rescue—Fiction. 2. Cats—Fiction. 3. Animals—Infancy—Fiction. 4. Sick—
Fiction. 5. Family life—Fiction.] I. Hulst, Willem G. van de (Willem Gerrit), 1917-
illustrator. II. Title.
PZ7.H887Bl 2014   [E]—dc23   2014017986

Originally published in Dutch as *Het zwarte poesje*
Cover painting and illustrations by Willem G. Van de Hulst, Jr.
Original translation done by Harry der Nederlanden for Paideia Press,
St. Catharines-Ontario-Canada.
The publisher expresses his appreciation to John Hultink of Paideia Press for
his generous permission to use his translation (ISBN 0-88815-507-7).

Edited by Paulina Janssen

ISBN 978-1-928136-07-1

Published simultaneously in U.S.A. by Inheritance Publications
Box 366, Pella, Iowa 50219

Printed in Canada

Contents

1. Up to the Bridge

"You may go up to the bridge, Sandy, but no farther. Do you hear?"

"Yes, Mother! Good-bye!"

Away went Sandy, at a trot. She had to run very fast. Sandy's brother and sister went to school early every morning. But not Sandy. She was still too young. But Mother said she was allowed to walk along with them a way — just a little way. Up to the bridge.

"Wait for me! Wait for me!" she cried.

"Hurry up, then!" Gerdie and Grant were already on the road. "Hurry up!"

It was hard for Sandy to run. The road was covered with deep snow and she was wearing wooden shoes. But Sandy was a big girl.

Slipping and sliding through the snow, she quickly caught up to Gerdie and Grant.

They let her walk between them.

"Shall we pull you, Sandy? Shall we?"

"Oh, yes!" Sandy sat down on her heels. Gerdie took her one hand and Grant the other. Together they pulled Sandy along. Her skirts dragged through the snow. What a wonderful ride!

Underneath the snow there was a big ugly stone. They did not see it on time and Sandy's little wooden shoes bumped right into the rock. Sandy tumbled forward; she rolled headfirst into the snow.

Brrr! Cold!

But Sandy was a big girl.

She laughed even though her knee hurt.

Away they went again. Gerdie and Grant were running and pulling her and they were going very fast.

Wonderful! Snow covered Sandy's face, but she didn't care.

Ahead was the bridge.

"Whoa!" Sandy shouted. "Whoa!"

She stayed behind, all alone.

Gerdie and Grant ran on. It was a long way to school.
Their lunch kits bounced along on their hips. They
couldn't come home at noon. The school was much
too far away.

"Good-bye!" they shouted. "Good-bye!"

"Good-bye!" Sandy shouted back.

"Will you meet us after school?" Gerdie yelled. "At
the bridge?"

"Yes!" shouted Sandy. "I will!"

Sandy was left behind, all alone.

It was bitterly cold. Mother had wrapped a thick scarf
around Sandy's neck and knotted it in the back, in a
big, lumpy knot. But the nasty wind nipped at her
red, swollen hands. So she hid them in her woolen
scarf, where it was nice and warm.

Sandy's curls were hidden deep under a red woolen
hat that was pulled down over her ears. The nasty
wind nipped at her red cheeks, but it couldn't reach
her ears. Not at all!

And Sandy was a big girl.

At a trot, she headed for home.

But the snow made icy lumps on the bottom of her wooden shoes. She couldn't run very fast; she almost stumbled. She wished she were back home. But bravely she went on, slipping and sliding.

Home! Where it was nice and warm. When she would get home, she would sit close to the stove. Mother would be folding the wash and she would let Sandy sort and fold Father and Grant's big red handkerchiefs. Wonderful!

Hurry, hurry! Home to the stove, to where it was warm and cozy. Hurry!

But those icy lumps on the bottom of her wooden shoes . . . Wait! She would stop and take them off a minute. Then she would . . .

2. The Foolish Little Kitten

Suddenly . . . !

Oh, look! A kitten! A cute little kitten! A black kitten in the white snow.

He was skipping and hopping across the road, his tail up in the air.

"Kitty! Here, kitty," Sandy called happily.

She forgot all about the big lumps under her shoes.

"Here, kitty! Come on, come to Sandy."

She crouched down to call the kitten better. But the playful little kitten didn't listen. Not at all. He skipped on. And when his little paws sank deep into the snow, he took a funny little hop high into the air.

All of a sudden, the kitten was gone.
The ground sloped a bit beside the canal and it was covered with snow. Did the little kitten go down the sloping bank, so frightfully close to the water?
"Here, kitty! You foolish little kitty!"
Sandy hobbled after him.
"Kitty! Be careful, kitty!" Yes, there he was, the foolish little kitten, right by the water. The water was covered with ice — a very thin layer of ice. And the wind had blown snow over it.
"Kitty! Come here, kitty! Oh, please come!"
Sandy went a little bit closer. Just a very little bit, because the ground sloped so steeply.

Oh, no! Her one foot slipped. And . . . thump! There she sat — in the snow on the sloping bank of the canal. And it was such a steep bank. One wooden shoe slipped off her foot and tumbled down the bank. The kitten was frightened. He didn't know what that strange thing tumbling down at him was. He thought it was pouncing at him. The kitten jumped out of the way.

Oh, no! Be careful, kitty. No, no, don't do it, you foolish little kitty. Don't go that way! No, not that way! There's water under there. You can't skip and hop over there. Be careful! Don't do it! That's not land. That's ice. It won't hold you. You foolish little kitty! No, no!

Oh, no! The foolish little kitten was so frightened by the wooden shoe, he jumped again. He jumped right onto the ice.

Crr-crr-crrack! Sploosh!

The poor little kitten! He thrashed about in the icy water. His little paws paddled wildly and he sputtered and sneezed and gasped for air. Oh, if his little head would go under water, then . . . !

Sandy was so terribly frightened.

"Oh, kitty, kitty!" she cried wildly. "Oh, kitty!"

But what did she do then? On her bottom she let herself slide down the bank. She would, she must, she had to save that poor little kitten. She would go and snatch him out of that icy black water. "Don't cry, kitty! Here I come!"

But, oh, no, she couldn't reach the kitten. She couldn't grab him; her arm was far too short. The little kitten thrashed and splashed and sputtered and paddled wildly with his little paws. He squealed in fear.

And Sandy? She didn't know what to do. There was no one else around, no one at all to help the little kitten.

Gerdie and Grant were long gone. There was no one on the road and there was no one in the fields. No one at all!

But all of a sudden she had an idea!

Yes, that's what she would do. She would hold her foot out over the water, the foot without a shoe. Then the kitty would be able to grab her sock with his tiny claws.

Yes, yes, that's what she would do! And then she would pull the poor little kitty out of the water. She

laid down flat on her back by the edge of the water. She held out the foot with the thick, black sock over the water, low over the water.
And the kitten? Yes, yes, it was working. The kitten grabbed the sock with his little paws.
Sandy felt his tiny claws. But she didn't care.
Hold on, kitty! Hold on!

Oh, no!
Poor little kitten!
Poor little Sandy!

3. The Man on the Motorcycle

Sandy slipped.
Just a little bit. But she couldn't hold her leg with the stocking foot up anymore. It dropped, but not into the water. It dropped right on top of the kitten. It pushed the poor little kitten under the water, head and all.
And then Sandy got another scare.
On the other side of the canal was a big, wide road.
Roaring down that road came a big motorcycle.
On it sat a man. His head was tucked down deep into the fur collar of his coat and a fur cap was pulled down over his ears.

The man saw Sandy's foot drop on top of the kitten. And he got terribly angry. He didn't know what had happened. He didn't know that Sandy was trying to help the little kitten.

No, he thought Sandy was teasing the poor little thing. He thought she was pushing it under the icy, black water with her foot on purpose. What a mean little girl! What a little rogue!

He shouted, "Stop that, you naughty little girl! Get out of there! Right now! Do you want to drown that poor kitten? Shame on you! Get out of there, you little rogue! Right now!"

Poor little Sandy!

It scared her terribly.

Her wet foot frightened her. The icy water shocked her. And the poor little kitten disappearing under the water scared her.

But most of all she was scared by the man who was scolding her. That voice, that roaring voice all of a sudden! It shouted that she, Sandy, was pushing the kitty into the water. And that wasn't true at all!

"Get out of there, you naughty little rogue!" the voice thundered again.

Poor little Sandy!

She got so terribly scared. She jumped up. She scrambled up the sloping side of the canal and started for home as fast as she could, a wooden shoe on one foot and a wet sock on the other.

"Mother, Mother!" she sobbed.

In her fright, she forgot all about the little kitten and her other wooden shoe. "Mother, Mother!"

Dripping wet, the little kitten scrambled out of the water by himself. He darted across the road, leaving a long trail of water droplets in the snow.

The man on the motorcycle rode on.

He noticed Sandy sneak a quick look back. That naughty little girl! Angrily he shook his fist at her, his fist with the big, black leather glove.

Poor little Sandy!

She burst into tears.

"It isn't true!" she sobbed. "It isn't true!"

4. Sandy Tells

Sandy reached home.

She crashed through the gate, slammed the door open, and threw herself into the room.

"Mother, Mother! It isn't true! It isn't true at all! I-I wanted to . . ."

Mother was standing by the table folding the wash. She looked up, startled.

"What? What's wrong, Sandy? And where's your other shoe? And your foot is all wet! Look, it's dripping on the floor. No, no, not on the carpet. Stay in the kitchen. I'll . . ."

"Mother, that man said . . . he said . . . and, Mother, it isn't true! It isn't! It isn't!" Sandy stamped on the floor with her wet foot so that water sprayed around the room. "It isn't true! It isn't!"

Mother had no idea what Sandy was talking about. She asked, "A man? What man? What happened, Sandy? Come here. First let me pull off those wet stockings. A wet foot in this cold weather! Do you want to get sick?"

Mother set Sandy on a chair and pulled off her socks. Then she rubbed her cold wet feet dry with a warm rag hanging by the stove.

Sandy told Mother what happened. She told her everything.

Mother listened.

"And then do you know what I did? I held out my foot over the water — stiff, like this. And it fell, but I couldn't help it. And then that man shouted at me. And it isn't true. It isn't true at all!"

Mother said, "Oh, that man didn't see it. Never mind him. Hush now. That man didn't know what he was talking about. Mother knows you wouldn't do that. You wanted to help that poor kitty, didn't you? But it was a little foolish of you to get so close to the water. You might have fallen in yourself!"

Mother gathered Sandy into her arms. "But you're my sweet, foolish little girl anyway! Come, first we'll take off that big scarf and that warm cap. And then you can help Mother with all those red hankies."

Soon Sandy had forgotten all about her fright.

She knelt on a chair by the table, close to the stove, and began to fold the red handkerchiefs very neatly.

Father was in the workshop, just off the kitchen. He was making wooden shoes. He sawed and chopped

and carved beautiful wooden shoes out of blocks of wood.

He whistled as he worked. Working hard and whistling happy tunes helped to keep him warm. He knew nothing about Sandy's big fright.

But when he put his head around the corner of the door, he saw a wet stocking hanging by the stove.

"What's that? What happened?"

Sandy's face clouded over again. Two big tears sprang into her eyes. "No, no!" she sobbed again. "It isn't true! It isn't true at all!"

Mother smiled a little and told Father what had happened.

Father smiled too. "Ah, my foolish little Sandy. Did you go fishing for kittens with your stocking foot? You foolish little kitten-catcher. I'll go right out and try to find your other wooden shoe. Or else I'll have to make you a new one."

Father left the house and hurried down the road.

He came back with the little wooden shoe. He had found it lying right beside the water, but he had seen nothing of the little kitten. Nowhere.

He did see the spot where the kitten climbed out of the water and he also saw the wet trail.

17

Father did not know where the kitten lived. He did not know who owned him.

Mother did not know either.

Sandy did not know at all.

"Oh, Mother, he was such a cute little kitty. He was all black and shiny-soft. And he had one white paw. So pretty!"

Father went back to his workshop. He planed and cut and chiselled beautiful wooden shoes out of blocks of wood — little wooden shoes and big wooden shoes. He whistled happy tunes as he worked. That kept him warm.

Mother began to peel potatoes. Sandy sat quietly by the stove. Even though it was nice and warm there, she shivered once in a while. Her wet stocking was dry again and was back on her foot. She was also wearing little slippers that Mother had made for her. Sandy huddled even closer to the stove. Cold shivers ran up and down her back.

Mother said, "You foolish little girl. You probably caught a cold sliding into that icy water with your foot. Brrr! I'll make you a cup of hot chocolate."

That afternoon Grant and Gerdie were on their way home from school. They were running home to meet Sandy.

"Shall we pull her along again on her wooden shoes?" Gerdie asked.

"Yes, yes," Grant said. "Let's go!" He pranced and tossed his head like a horse pulling a buggy.

But when they got to the bridge, Sandy wasn't there. Why not?

Too bad! They would have had such fun.

As they ran home, it was getting dark.

At home they would be able to huddle close to the stove.

And soon it would be suppertime. Applesauce and pork chops. Yummy!

They ran. They flew home like two little birds returning to their nest at nightfall.

5. In the Big Bed

It was dark outside, but inside the lights were on.
Father was reading in his big chair.
Mother was darning socks.
Gerdie was practising a song for school.
Grant was cutting paper dolls out of an old newspaper.
With a red crayon he was giving them all red hats, red noses, and red wooden shoes.
They were for Sandy, but Sandy wasn't playing with them.
"Sandy, let's play school!" Gerdie said.
But Sandy shook her head, "No." She sat at the table.
The stove was purring, but Sandy still shivered. Her cheeks were bright red, her head pounded, and her throat ached. She hadn't eaten the delicious applesauce and pork chops Mother had made for supper.
Mother looked at her.
Mother's eyes looked worried.
Mother said, "Sandy has a cold. Maybe because she got her foot wet. Sandy is a little sick. She has a fever."
Father looked at her too. He nodded. "Yes, Sandy is sick." Then he looked at the bed built into the wall, the bed with the pretty curtains. His eyes met Mother's, and Mother knew what he was thinking.

Then Mother said, "Sandy, listen! I have an idea. Tonight you may sleep in the big bed with Mother. Because you're a little bit sick. Won't that be nice?" Sleep in the big bed with Mother! That was very special!

The big bed that Father and Mother slept in was built into the wall of the living room. When you sat inside, the pretty green curtains around it made you feel like you were riding in a big coach pulled by six horses. And you could see and hear everything that was going on in the living room.

Sandy's eyes were bright with excitement.
In the big bed! Oh yes! Wouldn't that be cozy! She
hugged herself with excitement. "Oh, yes, Mother!
In the big bed!"
Father laughed. He would sleep upstairs that night
with Gerdie and Grant. And Sandy would stay
downstairs with Mother.
Grant thought, "I wish I was a little bit sick." He
looked at the green curtains and his scissors slipped.
He cut the head right off his paper doll.

"Well, Sandy, shall I tuck you away in the big coach?
I'll leave the curtains open," Mother said.
"Yes! Oh yes!" said Sandy. Her voice was hoarse
and her throat ached. Her eyes sparkled and her
cheeks glowed. Partly because she had a fever. And
partly because she was so excited.

6. How Strange!

It was nighttime.
A small lamp was burning on the mantel.
Mother was sleeping in the front of the big bed and
Sandy was sleeping by the wall.
Sandy was snuggled tightly against Mother, warm and
cozy.

Mother had taken Sandy's little hands in hers. That was how Sandy had said her bedtime prayer.

Mother prayed too. She whispered, but Sandy could hear it. And Sandy knew that the Lord in Heaven could hear it too, no matter how softly Mother spoke. The Lord knew everything and saw everything and heard everything. The Lord also knew that Sandy was sick.

Suddenly Sandy thought of something very beautiful. Since the Lord knew everything, He also knew that she did not push that poor kitten under the water.

Mother and Sandy laid down to sleep. Mother was like a big mountain and Sandy hid behind her.
Then she could not fall into the icy water. Then the man on the motorcycle couldn't get her or shout at her. He couldn't even find her. Was that a little kitten under the blankets? Was it scratching her toes?
She felt strange, so strange. Her head pounded and her throat ached.
She snuggled even closer to Mother's shoulder.

But then . . .

Suddenly she was walking by the bridge — barefoot in the snow. How strange! She heard a kitten meow

but she didn't know where he was.

She started to look for him. She looked under the bridge and under the bushes. She also looked in the water. Oh, no! There, there he was. There, deep down under the water. How strange! How horrible! The kitten put up his little white paw as if to say, "Help me! Help me, please!" His nose was red just like the noses on Grant's paper dolls. How strange!

But suddenly . . . oh, no!

The man on the motorcycle roared up behind her.

He wore huge, red wooden shoes, just like Grant's paper dolls. He shouted and thundered.

He grabbed her by her nightgown with his big, black leather gloves. "You naughty little girl! You little rogue! Did you push another kitten into the water? You're coming with me!"

"No, no!" Sandy sobbed. "No, it isn't true! It isn't true at all!"

But then he put her on the back of the motorcycle.

And then . . . How strange! How terrible! He took a little kitten out of his coat pocket, a shiny black kitten with one white paw. And out of his other pocket he took another kitten. And then another.

More and more kittens. His pockets were full of them. He put them all down on the road in front of the motorcycle and made them pull him along.

"Giddyup! Giddyup!"

And off they went. Sandy sat behind the man on the back of his motorcycle.

She had to go along. They went faster and faster. The kittens ran and hopped out in front, their tails up in the air. The motorcycle snarled and growled and grumbled.

They rode onto the ice. The ice cracked, cracked!

Sandy was very frightened. She didn't want to go along. She wanted to get off. She pounded on the man's dark back. She pounded and pounded with both her hands. "Let me off! Let me off!" She screamed in fear. She pounded and kicked.

"Sandy, Sandy! What are you doing? Why are you pounding and kicking me so? Sandy, wake up!" Mother gently shook Sandy from side to side.

Then Sandy opened her eyes.

She looked around. She saw the small lamp on the mantel, she saw the curtains of the big bed, and she also saw Mother. "Oh, Mother, Mother!" She threw her arms around Mother's neck. "Oh, Mother, he had all those kittens in his pockets and he made me go along!"

"It's all right. It's all right. You were just dreaming. You are in bed with Mother, safe and sound. No one will hurt you. Silly girl, you were pounding and kicking your own mother. But it was just a dream. It's all over now.

"Would you like a drink? Some honey tea to make your throat feel better?"
Then, cuddled together in each other's arms, they went back to sleep.

7. The Doctor

The next morning . . .
Sandy was very sick. She needed a doctor. The old doctor in the village had moved to the city and another doctor was living in his house.
Father went to the new doctor.
"Doctor, our Sandy is very sick," Father said.
And the doctor replied, "I'll come and take a look at your little girl right away."

That afternoon . . .
Sandy was lying in the big bed, buried deep under the blankets.
With one eye she peeked past the edge of her pillow into the living room. She could just see through the window into the quiet, white world outside.
Listen! From far away came a soft hum. Listen!
The humming was getting closer and louder. Listen!
It turned into the roar of a motorcycle. It suddenly stopped, right by the window. A man got off. His

head was tucked down deep into the fur collar of his coat and a fur cap was pulled down over his ears. He clapped his hands together to warm them up.

He was wearing big, black leather gloves.
Sandy could just see him with one eye. "Oh!"

Listen! There was a knock on the door. Listen!
The door opened and that . . . that strange man came right into the room.
Sandy saw him come in. Her heart pounded with fright. It . . . he . . . that . . . that was the man on the motorcycle!
"Oh!"

Mother was sitting at the table. She stood up.
Father came in from his workshop.
The man with the fur cap said, "Good afternoon. And where is the sick little girl?" He took off his gloves. He had a friendly face. Then he came toward the big bed.

Poor, poor Sandy!
She didn't see the friendly face. She hid deep down under the blankets.
She shivered with fear. Her hoarse little voice

squeaked, "No, no! It isn't true! I didn't do it, I didn't!"

Mother saw; Mother understood.

The new doctor must have been the man on the motorcycle, the man who had scared Sandy so terribly. And now that same man walked right into their house.

And he stood right by Sandy's bed.

Mother said, "Oh, Doctor, Sandy is scared of you."

The doctor laughed, "Scared of me? Not really! Why? How come you're hiding so deep down under the blankets, you silly little girl? Do you think I can't find you in your warm little nest?"

He pulled back the covers. But then Sandy flew up and scrambled away, scrambled to the far corner of the bed with her eyes wild. "No, no!" wheezed her hoarse little voice. "No, no! I didn't do it! I didn't! It isn't true!"

Big tears rolled down her cheeks. Her little hands clutched her nightgown in fear.

The doctor shook his head. He didn't understand at all. He said, "What's wrong? Why is she so scared of me?"

"You see, Doctor," Mother said, "you see, it's because you scolded her so terribly."

"Who, me? I scolded her? That can't be. I've never seen her before."

"Yes, Doctor, you did."

"But where?"

"By the little bridge. Yesterday. With the little kitten."
The doctor's eyebrows went up. "Ah, now I see!"
he said. "She was the naughty little girl by the
bridge."

"No, no!" sobbed Sandy. "No, no! It isn't true!"
She pushed her face into the blanket. "It isn't true at
all!"

"No, Doctor. She wasn't a naughty girl. Really, she
wasn't," said Mother. "She wasn't teasing the kitten.
She was trying to help it. Shall I tell you the whole
story?"

"Yes, please do!" said the doctor. "Tell me everything."

And Mother told him about the kitten, and about the sloping bank of the canal, and about the wooden shoe, and about Sandy's stocking foot that fell down on the kitten. She told him that Sandy really couldn't help it. That she loved the pretty little kitten.

"Well, well!" said the doctor. "So that's what happened! I didn't know."

"Yes, Doctor. She was only trying to help."

"Then she's a fine girl, a brave girl. And I'm a foolish doctor. Did I scare you so badly? That wasn't right! That wasn't fair! I'm sorry I scolded you."

"Now, back under the blankets, Sandy," said Mother. Sandy crawled out of her far corner, back to her warm little nest in the front of the bed.

She still sobbed a little, but her fear was already starting to go away.

"There, there!" said the doctor. "Come here. You need not be afraid of me. I won't hurt you or scold you. Did you want to help that poor little kitten? That's good. That's very good! And did your one foot drop into that icy water? That's not good. Not good at all! That icy water might have made you sick. Now I'm going to look at your throat. Open wide. No, first dry those tears, all right? Now we'll be good friends. Right? There, there! Now it's all good."

Then Sandy saw that the doctor had a very friendly face. Slowly her fear went away.

"Are you angry with me?" asked the doctor.

"No," Sandy shook her head.

"Aren't you at all angry anymore with the foolish doctor who scolded you so?"

"No, no," Sandy shook her head and smiled.

"I'll give you a little bottle of medicine to make you feel better. And you'll have to stay deep under the blankets. And listen, if I see that black kitten along the road, I'll tell him you're a good girl. And that you weren't trying to tease him, but to help him. And that I was a foolish doctor. Good-bye now! I'll be back again soon. Be sure to stay under the blankets."

8. Sandy is Sick

Again it was nighttime.

The lamp burned, but it looked as if the lamp was sad.

It was very quiet in the small living room.

Grant was drawing.

Gerdie was knitting.

Mother was mending a hole in Grant's pants.

Father was reading the newspaper, but every so often he looked over at the big bed.

Grant wanted to show off his drawing. It was a haystack.

"Shhh! Quiet!" Mother whispered. "I think Sandy is sleeping. The doctor said she is very sick."

Sandy moaned in her sleep. She wheezed as she breathed. Her cheeks burned with fever.

Sometimes she tossed and turned under the blankets.

Again and again the four at the table looked over at the big bed — Father, Mother, Gerdie, and Grant. They looked sad. They couldn't do anything to help sick little Sandy.

The little bottle of medicine stood on a chair by the pretty curtains.

It was a very quiet, sad evening.

When bedtime came, Mother knelt in the dark and prayed for Sandy. Sandy couldn't say her prayers herself. She was too sick.

Upstairs Father also prayed for his sick little girl. Gerdie and Grant knelt beside their beds. Then they quickly dove under the blankets. They heard Sandy moan downstairs. And deep under the blankets, all alone, they said another silent little prayer for their sick little sister. God hears silent prayers too.

The doctor came every day. But he didn't joke with Sandy. She was much too sick. "Make sure she takes her medicine," he said.

Once in awhile there was a soft knock at the door and a short little man would come in. He was the old farmer who lived by the bridge. He was always cheerful, but his lower lip was crooked. That was because of the curved little pipe that always dangled from his mouth.

"Hmm! Hmm!" he said softly.

He looked at the big bed and put a few eggs on the table. They were for Sandy, to make her strong again.

"Ho, my brave little missy," he said softly, "are you so sick?" Then he left again, his curved little pipe dangling from his crooked lip. His name was Farmer Klomp.

9. The Secret

One beautiful morning when the sun was shining, the doctor came again. He was wearing his hat today.

His fur cap was home in the closet. The cold wind, the snow that had been on the ground, the ice that had been on the water, were all gone. The warm sun had chased them away.

The doctor felt Sandy's pulse and peered down her throat. He looked very friendly and pleased. He patted Sandy's cheek. "You're a good girl. You took your medicine well."

To Father and Mother he said, "Good news! She's starting to get better. She may sit up in bed for awhile every day with some pillows behind her back."

"Oh, Doctor!" Mother said. She was very happy.

For the first time in a long time, Father whistled a tune in his workshop, but very softly. He was very happy too.

Gerdie and Grant were at school.

They had not heard the good news yet.

The doctor left. He came to the bridge.

Beep-beep! Look out! Careful, you little rascal!

A little black kitten was playing beside the canal.

Suddenly he flew across the road, right in front of the motorcycle, almost under the front wheel.

The little rascal!

The doctor slammed his brakes. Then he saw which little kitten it was.

Is that you, you little rascal? Sure enough, all black with one white paw. Were you going for another swim? The little kitten was very frightened by that big noisy thing on the road.

He scurried away through the dead leaves and under the bushes.

And the doctor? He switched off his motorcycle and jumped off. "Where did you go so quickly, you little black fuzzball?"

The doctor looked under the leaves, but he couldn't find the kitten.

He looked in the bare orchard, but he couldn't find the kitten anywhere. "Where did you go, you little blackie?"

The doctor smiled. "You've given me an idea, you little clown. A wonderful idea!"

He passed through the gate, through the orchard to the white farmhouse. It was Farmer Klomp's house. The old farmer was sitting outside in the sunshine. He had a cheerful look on his face, but his lower lip was crooked. That was because of the curved little pipe that always dangled from his mouth.

The doctor said, "Farmer Klomp, I've come to make a deal. I'd like to buy one of your animals."

"An animal, Doctor? Fine, fine! What kind of animal do you want? A nice fat pig?"

"No, not a pig."

"Some chickens?"

"No, no chickens."

"You want my dog?"

"No, not your dog either. I want to buy a kitten — the little black kitten with one white paw."

"Ha-ha-ha! The kitten! Fine, fine! But I don't want to sell it. No, Doctor. I've got two other cats around the place. I'll give you the kitten. Do you have mice in your home, Doctor? Do you want him for catching mice?"

"No, not for that. It's a secret."

Together the doctor and the old farmer went out to look for the kitten.

It was playing in the haystack. The hay tickled his nose. So the kitten bit at it and swatted it with his white paw.

Farmer Klomp tried to grab him. Missed! The doctor tried to grab him. And he got him!

The kitten was frightened by those big men and their big hands. But when he found himself in the doctor's arms, he was happy. He purred with happiness.

"All right, little fuzzball, you're coming with me."

"Do you have a basket to put the kitten in, Doctor?"

"A basket? No, I don't. But I've got a good spot for him. I can take him with me. See?"

The doctor was still wearing his big winter coat, the coat with two big pockets.

And what did that funny doctor do? He put the little kitten in his big coat pocket. "That should be a safe spot. He can't fall out of there."

The old farmer laughed, "Yes, yes! Fine, fine! And what are you going to do with the little kitten?"

"That's a secret."

10. Just Like the Dream

Sandy was sitting up in the big bed with some pillows behind her back.

Her cheeks had become very pale and her little hands very thin, but she was happy that she could sit up and look around the room. Now she could also see outside through the window. But where was all the snow?

Shhh! She heard something outside.

She also saw something.

It was the doctor. He was coming into the house and there was a huge smile on his face. Why?

Mother hurried to meet him. She looked at him in surprise. Why did the doctor come back?

And why was he winking at her?

He stepped toward the big bed.

He said, "Hello, Sandy! Can you guess what I've got in my pocket?" He held the pocket of his big coat open just a crack. How strange! Was Sandy supposed to look inside the doctor's pocket? Why?

Sandy tipped her head a little. Then she saw something black, something shiny-soft with a white spot. It was moving!

All of a sudden . . . Sandy's pale cheeks turned pink at the sight. All of a sudden, out of the big coat pocket came a cute little head, with two twinkling little eyes, a pink little nose, and a pink tongue.

The doctor's big hand lifted the little kitten out of
the pocket very carefully.

And then he put the little kitten right on Sandy's lap.

"There you go. He's all yours!"

And Sandy? Her eyes sparkled and her thin little hands
reached out. Oh, the kitten!

"Mother, Mother, the kitty!"

The doctor laughed. Mother said, "Oh, Sandy!"

And Father peeked around the corner of the door.

Sandy petted the little kitten and hugged him.

"Out of your pocket!" she said. "A kitty out of your
pocket just like in my dream!"

"Your dream?" The doctor sat down on the chair by
the bed. He put the little bottle of medicine up on the
mantel.

"Your dream? Did you dream about the kitten?"

Then Sandy told him the dream. She told him that he had made her come along on the motorcycle. That she had been very frightened. That he had taken more and more kittens out of his pockets. That they had to pull his motorcycle and that they went faster and faster.

The doctor laughed aloud.

He said, "So, you little dreamer! And now your dream came true! A kitten out of my pocket. But now you're not scared of the man on the motorcycle anymore, are you? And you're not angry at him anymore, are you? Now you may keep the kitten. Make sure you take good care of him. Good-bye!"

The doctor left.

Sandy played with her kitten for a while until the little fuzzball fell asleep curled up on the blankets.

He lay against Sandy's hand, warm and soft. Sandy kept her hand very still.

There was a soft knock at the door. A short, little man came in. "Hmmm! Hmmm!" he said softly.

And he put three eggs on the table — for Sandy. He looked at the big bed. He saw that Sandy was sitting up and that her eyes were sparkling happily.

"Fine, fine! Ho, my brave little missy, are you starting to get better?"

And then he saw something else.

There, curled up on the blankets. His cheerful face

became even more cheerful, and the curved little pipe danced up and down in the corner of his crooked lip. "Ah-ha!" he said. "Ah-ha! So that  was the doctor's secret! Fine, fine! Yes, that's good. Excellent! Be sure to take good care of your kitty, my little missy."

He shuffled off, his curved pipe dangling from his mouth.

11. "We Thank Thee"

When darkness came and the lamp was lit, Father and Mother, Gerdie and Grant sat at the table. Sandy lay in the big bed watching and listening. It was so warm and cozy. Her head was not pounding anymore and her throat did not ache anymore.

Grant was drawing a motorcycle for her, with red wheels and red handlebars.

Sandy couldn't keep her eyes open.

"Shhh! Quiet!" whispered Mother. "Sandy is sleeping. Don't wake her up."

They looked over at the big bed — Father, Mother,

Gerdie, and Grant. But this time their eyes weren't sad.

They were all glad, very glad. Sandy was getting better.

"Meow! Meow!"

From under the table came a soft little voice.

Mother picked up the little kitten. "Yes, you're right, you're part of the family too now."

The kitten snuggled down on Mother's lap under her sewing. That was a warm, cozy spot.

It was a quiet, but a very, very happy evening.

Later that night, when Mother came to bed too, Sandy woke up. Mother told her how the kitten had slept on her lap.

Now it was lying on an old blanket beside the stove.

Before they went to sleep, Mother took Sandy's little hands between her big hands and they prayed together. Mother whispered and Sandy listened.

Mother said, "Dear Lord, we are so happy — all of us. Thou hast made Sandy better. Thou hast made the medicine help. We thank Thee. Please make Sandy strong again. And, dear Lord, make us all love Thee."

Cuddled close together, Mother and Sandy went to sleep. The little black kitten rolled over on his blanket. The moon shone on his black back.

12. A Party

Spring had come.
The cold winter, with its snow and its biting wind and its freezing rain, was gone.
The sun shone, the flowers bloomed, and the birds chirped and twittered in the sky.

Sandy was all better.
The medicine in her little bottle was all gone. Mother let her drink lemonade out of the little bottle.
The doctor no longer stopped at the little house.

Sandy played outside in the sunshine. When Gerdie and Grant went to school, she went with them as far as the bridge. Sometimes the little black kitten went skipping along and he came skipping back home with her too.

"Careful! Don't go near the water. This way!"

Sometimes Farmer Klomp was standing by his gate. Then he would nod cheerfully at Sandy. He smiled and the curved pipe danced in his mouth. "You take good care of your kitty, little missy."

One sunny afternoon, the doctor once again came riding down the road on his motorcycle.

Sandy was playing along the road.

Father was working behind the house and whistling a happy tune.

The doctor got off his motorcycle. And what did he do next, that funny doctor? He grabbed Sandy and he set her behind him on the back of the motorcycle. "Hold on to the bar. You're coming along with me. We're going for a ride — you and I."

Mother put her head out the open window.

The doctor shouted, "Don't worry, Mother. I'll be very careful. We're going for a little ride on the motorcycle. We'll be right back. Sandy's scary dream is going to become a happy dream."

Vrrroom, vrrroom! Away they went. Sandy's eyes sparkled with excitement. She held the bar very tightly with her little hands. Vrrroom!

The little black kitten skipped ahead in front of the motorcycle.

"Look, look!" cried the doctor laughing. "Just like in the dream! The kitten is pulling us. Ha-ha-ha!"

But the kitten got scared of the noisy thing behind him. He darted off the road and climbed a tree.

Vrrroom! Oh, wonderful! It was a wonderful ride. Over the little bridge, down the big road, to the village they went. They stopped at the bakery and the doctor bought a bag of tiny gingerbread cookies — for Sandy. Then they headed back for home. Vrrroom, vrrroom!

Grant and Gerdie were just on their way home from school. They were walking by the bridge when the motorcycle came down the road. As it passed them, who did they see sitting on the back of the motorcycle?

"Sandy! Sandy!" they shouted as loudly as they could. "Sandy!" They ran after the motorcycle, but they couldn't keep up. Sandy couldn't hear them and she didn't dare look back. She was riding so fast, so wonderfully fast.

And that evening . . .
Father and Mother, Grant and Gerdie, and Sandy sat around the table. Sandy shared her cookies with everyone. What a wonderful party it was.
And who was sitting under the table nibbling along? The little black kitten.

Titles in this series:

1. The Little Wooden Shoe
2. Through the Thunderstorm
3. Bruno the Bear
4. The Basket
5. Lost in the Snow
6. Annie and the Goat
7. The Black Kitten
8. The Woods beyond the Wall
9. My Master and I
10. The Pig under the Pew
11. Three Little Hunters
12. The Search for Christmas
13. Footprints in the Snow
14. Little Tramp
15. Three Foolish Sisters
16. The Secret Hiding Place
17. The Secret in the Box
18. The Rockity Rowboat
19. Herbie, the Runaway Duck
20. Kittens, Kittens Everywhere
21. The Forbidden Path